Michelle Harrison

Midnight Magic

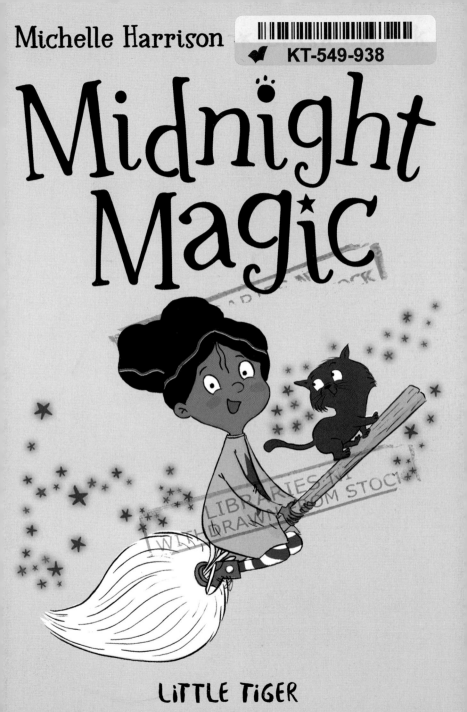

LiTTLE TiGER

LONDON

Chapter One

One frosty evening,
A tabby cat prowled
Through white winter fields
While a bitter wind howled.

Led by the moonlight
She slunk up a hill
And crept in a barn,
Escaping the chill.

Her tummy was heavy,
Each step made it jiggle
And there deep inside it
She felt something wriggle.

The horses stood by
As she fluffed up some straw
Then curled up and had
A good wash with her paw.

With that, she was ready
And so, with a mew,
Appeared a white kitten
All downy and new.

The mother cat licked it,
Outside the wind blew
And in the next heartbeat
One kitten was two.

The second was black
With four snow-white socks
And a big bushy tail
A bit like a fox.

The two furry bundles
Nuzzling and dozy
Burrowed down into
The straw, snug and cosy.

"Snowdrop's your name,"
Mum proudly said,
Swatting a flea
From the white kitten's head.

"And you I'll call Foxy,"
She said to the other.
"Snowdrop, my darling,
Meet your new brother!"

Outside, thunder **rumbled**
And rain **pounded** the door.
As midnight arrived
So did one kitten more.

Her purr was melodic,
Her claws tiny crescents
All wrapped in black fur —
A velvety present.

Eyes **green** and **rascally**!
Thoughts that were **cheeky**!
Paws full of **pounces**,
And plans **smart** and **sneaky**!

"I'll call you Midnight,"

Mum said in a whisper

Then gasped as smoke puffed

Out of black kitty's whiskers.

It curled into corners
And swept through the barn,
Twisting and turning
Like long purple yarn.

It looped round a broom
With a strong horsy smell,

Ruffling its bristles,

Casting a spell...

The broom started moving!
It shot in the air
As though it were normal
For it to be there.

It swooped in the rafters,
It danced with the rats,
It did loop the loop
With a trio of bats.

The horses were puzzled
But mother cat guessed
That one of her kittens
Was not like the rest.

Black cats born at midnight
Are different indeed,
A mischievous, odd
And peculiar breed.

For in every whisker
And each tuft of fur,
In every pounce
And every purr...

There's magic (yes, **MAGIC!**)
And strong stuff at that!

And Midnight was one
Of these rare types of cat.

She watched with delight
As the bumbling broom
Blasted straight up through
The roof to the moon.

It circled the stars
And danced till first light
And only came back
After picking a fight...

With a scarecrow nearby
(A bit of a grump —
Though rogue brooms could
Surely make anyone jump).

The hole in the roof
That the broomstick had ripped
Began leaking water —
It dribbled and dripped!

Snowdrop and Foxy
Both shivered and sneezed
While mother cat **hissed** at
The broom, far from pleased!

Midnight, however,
Was wide-eyed with wonder.
Could this be a friend,
Despite the broom's blunder?

It lurked in a corner
Pretending to sweep
Then sneaked a bit nearer
Once all were asleep.

The kittens slept late,
Not stirring till noon,
Two with their mother
And one with the broom.

Mother cat knew then
What she had to do
But kept it a secret...
She'd wait till they grew.

While Foxy and Snowdrop
Were learning to hunt,
Midnight would practise
Her latest broom stunt.

"Oh, Snowdrop! Foxy!"
She'd call from up high.
"This is such fun!
Won't you please learn to fly?"

But try as they might
They found that they couldn't

While mother cat frowned,
Hissing, **"Good kittens shouldn't!"**

The kittens chased tails
Or played hide-and-seek
But Midnight could easily
Hide for a week.

She'd vanish completely
Or shrink like a pea.
(Not cheating exactly
But still hard to see.)

Chapter Two

With each passing day
Midnight's magic would **double**.
Mother cat realized
They'd soon land in **trouble**.

One day Midnight woke
And searched ... and then wept.
Her mother and siblings
Had left while she slept.

Snowdrop and Foxy
And Mother were *gone!*
Abandoning her
As she'd slumbered on.

"I'll manage," she said,
Trying hard not to cry.
The broom shuffled closer
And dabbed her eyes dry.

When Midnight stopped sniffling
She said, "Time to go."
Quite where, she thought sadly,
She didn't yet know.

She crossed sunny meadows

Where all was in bloom

And not far behind her
There followed the broom.

"Go back," Midnight told it.
"You can't come with me.
I'm trouble, no good,
A cat-astrophe!"

Strangely, the broom only
Found this inviting.
Life with *this* cat
Would be very exciting!

Midnight decided
It should have a name.
"'Twiggy' is perfect.
I'm so glad you came!"

So Midnight and Twiggy
Travelled all day
And found an old village
Some distance away.

"It's not long till dark,"
Midnight was saying
But stopped as she noticed
A child nearby playing.

The girl spotted Midnight,
Instantly smitten.
"Ooooh!" she squealed. **"Look!
A beautiful kitten!"**

She scooped Midnight up
And was tickling her chin
When a deep voice called out:
"Trixie! Time to come in!"

I like her, thought Midnight.
She seems sweet and kind.
They skipped to a house
With the broom right behind.

In bounded Trixie
While Twiggy hung back...
Too late! The broom met
With a furry attack!

Doodle the dog was
So bouncy and plump
He knocked Twiggy over:

Clash!

Rattle!

Bang!

Thump!

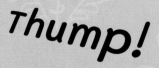

"Crumbs!" shouted Dad.
"What a hullabaloo!"
He rushed towards Trixie
Then saw Midnight too.

"What's *that*?" Dad demanded,
"That black ball of fluff?"
"Oh, Dad," Trixie pleaded.
"Don't get in a huff...

"This poor little cat
Was outside, all alone.
Please let me keep her,
Let's give her a home!"

"Aren't black cats unlucky?"
Dad pondered uncertain,
Imagining 'presents'
And claw-shredded curtains.

"She'd scare off the rats!"
Trixie protested.
"I heard you tell Nan
That the cellar's infested!"

Just then Nan returned
From her horse-riding class
With straw in her hair
And all covered in grass.

"Coo!" Nan said, grinning.
"We needed a cat!"
"She'd better behave, though,"
Dad said. "And that's that!"

Meanwhile, poor Twiggy
Was covered in licks
And gnawed on and nibbled
And chewed like a stick.

"What's this old broom?" Nan said,
Going to chuck it
Deep in the store cupboard
Next to a bucket.

They gave Midnight milk
In a porcelain dish
And little brown biscuits
That tasted of fish.

Then Dad tapped his watch.
"Uh-oh!" Trixie said.
"Come on, you!" Dad sighed.
"Bath, book and then **BED!**"

So Nan filled the bathtub
And Trixie hopped in
The frothy white bubbles
Right up to her chin.

Perched on the edge,
Midnight gazed at the water
Then almost slipped off...
Before Trixie caught her.

Perhaps there's a way,
Midnight thought, *to say thanks*
For taking me in...
Ah, I'll show her some **pranks!**

She wiggled her tail
And from it burst out
A thick jet of smoke
That zigzagged about.

It turned the air purple

Like thick witch's brew,

Circling bubbles

To streak past the loo.

Midnight leaped on to
A bubble mid-air
Then jumped right *inside*
And did somersaults there.

"Amazing!" cried Trixie,
Clapping and squealing.
The feline-filled bubble
Bounced clean off the ceiling!

From bubble to bubble
Our Midnight would hop,
Choosing a new one
Then making it ‑ **POP!** ‑

With each pop the floor
Became wetter and wetter,
Yet still Midnight wanted
To do something better...

Chapter
Three

A twitch of her tail
Sent a seahorse-shaped comb
Harrumphing to life
As it dived in the foam.

Next Midnight winked at
A duck on the side.
It quacked and slid down
Trixie's legs like a slide.

"Make me a **mermaid!**"
Trixie yelled, grinning,
As the seahorse and duck
Did some synchronized swimming.

"What's all that **racket**?"
Dad called from next door
While grabbing pyjamas
From Trixie's top drawer.

"Nothing!" cried Trixie
(To put Dad at ease).
To Midnight she whispered,
"I'd like a tail, please!"

Midnight got ready
To grant the request...
But then Dad came in
And became quite distressed.

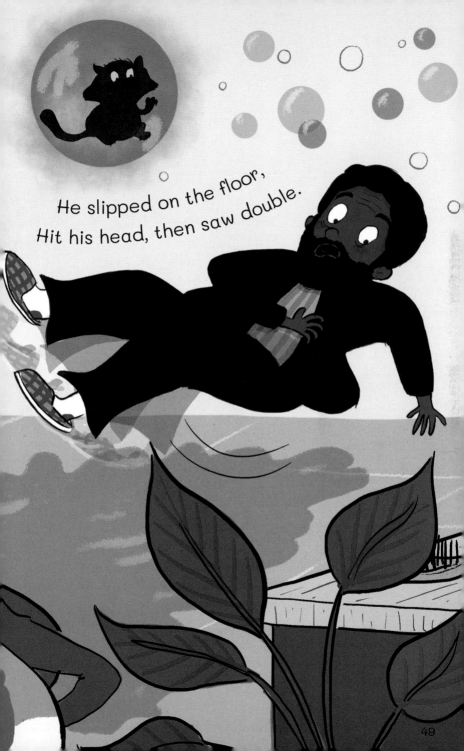

He slipped on the floor,
Hit his head, then saw double.

49

Midnight jumped down
Just before Nan appeared.
Dad scrambled up and
Stood scratching his beard.

He muttered, "There's something
Not right with that moggy!"
"It's true," Nan agreed,
"Cats hate getting soggy."

"No, it was *floating*.
I *saw* it!" Dad said.
"Yes!" Trixie snorted.
"When you bumped your head!"

Soon she was dry
And in her pyjamas.
Dad declared, "Bed!
And *please*, no more dramas."

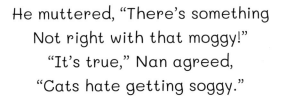

So Nan read a tale
From *Arabian Nights*;
Of genies in bottles
And carpets in flight.

"Another!" begged Trixie,
Concealing her yawns.
"The one with the castle
Surrounded by thorns."

Perched on the bed
Keeping Trixie's feet snug,
Midnight glanced naughtily
Down at the rug.

She noticed the wallpaper
Covered in flowers
(A bit like the book
But without castle towers).

*Now this could be **FUN***!
Midnight thought to herself,
As the books were returned
To their place on the shelf.

"Sweet dreams," whispered Nan,
Kissing Trixie goodnight.
She pulled the door shut
After dimming the light.

But it wasn't quite dark —
Smoke crept through the room.
The rug started rippling...
The walls were in bloom!

Trixie sat upright,
Awake and enthralled
As branches and brambles
Twisted and sprawled.

In moments the bedroom
Was perfumed by roses
Of white, pink and red
Growing under their noses.

"It's just like the tale!"
Trixie said with a gasp,
Aware that the carpet
Was vanishing fast.

The rug took its chance
To leap into flight,
Swooping and soaring
Above at great height.

It swooped low to flutter
Down by Trixie's side
To let her and Midnight
Climb on for a ride.

They looped upside down
While holding on tight,
Avoiding the prickles
And dodging the light.

TRIXIE's
ROOM

The brambles kept growing
With roses galore.
Where could they go
Except out of the door...?

Midnight's fur rippled:
Their speed had increased!
They hurtled downstairs
Like the rug had been greased!

Dipping past Doodle
Trix patted his head.
But scatty old Doodle —
He whimpered and fled!

They flew through the living room
Skimming Dad's hair.
He spat out his tea
And fell right off his chair.

Dad hiccupped and squeaked
(Sounding very high-pitched),
"Trix, come down at once!
That kitten's **bewitched!**"

Plop! went Nan's biscuit
And sank in her tea.
"Wait!" she called gleefully.
"Make room for me!"

Dad lunged for the rug
Then gasped as he saw
Roses and thorns
Spreading over the floor.

They'd spilled down the stairs
And were filling the hall,
Snagging on curtains,
Creeping up walls!

"Crumbs," Trixie muttered.
"We *are* in a pickle."
Midnight agreed as
Dad stepped on a prickle.

Chapter
Four

They flew through the kitchen
With Dad in pursuit
And landed before
Any brambles took root.

Dad leaped on Trixie
To give her a hug
And then said to Midnight
(Still sat on the rug):

"Small girls shouldn't fly
And neither should cats!
They sleep or climb trees
And go off chasing rats!"

"Rubbish!" Nan shouted.
"No magical cat
Is happy to do things
As boring as that!

"When I was a nipper
I had one the same.
We had such adventures!
Winks was his name."

Then from the cupboard
A **rat-a-tat** sounded.
"Now who could that be?"
Trixie wondered, astounded.

Dad opened the door
And out Twiggy flew.
"Hurrah!" Nan exclaimed.
"The broom's alive too!"

Midnight jumped on
As Twig hovered low.
Nan swung her leg over
Raring to go.

"Come on, Trix!" she yelled.
Dad said, "I think **not**!
No seat belts or brakes?
Your nan's a crackpot!"

"Oh, Dad!" Trixie giggled.
"Stop making a fuss.
OF COURSE we'll be safe
Because *you'll* be with us!"

So Dad clambered on
Looking frightfully green.
He perched behind Nan
Squeezing Trix in between.

"Don't worry," said Nan.
"I've done this before."
She yelled, "Giddy up!"
And Twig zoomed to the door.

It dropped like a drawbridge!
The moon was in sight!
So Twig and four riders
Flew into the night.

It was then Midnight saw
The extent of her powers.
For now Trixie's house was
A castle with towers!

Below its grand turrets
And walls of grey stone,
Rose petals dotted
A moat of its own.

"It's super!" cried Trixie.
"The best castle **EVER!**"
(And even Dad had to
Admit it was clever.)

"This broomstick," he added,
Now looking less queasy,
"Would mean no more traffic jams.
Flying is easy!

"And Midnight's a marvel!
Who wants a rat-catcher?
Some average puss,
A furniture scratcher?"

Midnight **purred** joyfully,
Trixie was cheering,
Nan whooped and almost
Forgot she was steering.

They swerved past the castle
Avoiding collision.
(Amazing, considering
Nan's dodgy vision.)

"Your spectacles, quick!"
Dad bellowed in fear.
Nan reached in her pocket.
"Chill out, dear, they're here!"

"Higher!" urged Trixie
As Nan cackled, "Faster!"
Dad gnashed his teeth,
Sure they'd meet with disaster.

They soared over rooftops

And rivers and bridges

Pointing out glow-worms

And spitting out midges.

They whooshed through a tunnel,
Damp, dark and twisty.
Emerging, Nan mumbled,
"Me specs have gone misty!"

Then "Duck!" hollered Trixie.
"A *duck*?" Dad asked. "Where?
No ducks are nocturnal
That I am aware——"

"No, **DUCK!**" Trix repeated
As trees loomed ahead.
Dad went to speak
But was silenced instead...

For right in his chops
An apple went ***smack!***
Luckily, Braeburns
Were Dad's favourite snack!

They flew high and low
Until Trixie was yawning.
So Midnight said, "Home, Twig.
It's not long till morning."

Once back it was clear
As the night slipped away
That their castle appeared
Rather flashy by day.

"Blimey," Nan muttered
As Dad said, "Oh, gosh!
Our cottage was cosier.
This is too posh!"

Crumbs, Midnight thought,
I got carried away!
As Trixie said sadly,
"I wish it could stay."

But Nan wagged her finger
And said with great sorrow,
"We'd have every newspaper
Camped here tomorrow!

"It has to change back
Without further ado.
Besides, all the neighbours
Would ask for one too!"

The castle looked splendid
And jolly good fun
But Midnight knew that
Her spell must be undone.

And so with a mew
And a magical wink
The castle transformed
To a house in a blink.

Gone were the brambles,
The roses no more,
The rug now behaving
Itself on the floor.

I did it! thought Midnight.
*My magic's so strong!
And now I'm in charge
Of it, I can't go wrong!*

Twig stayed downstairs
In the cupboard all snug
While Dad and Nan gave
Trix a big bedtime hug.

Trixie and Midnight
Both hopped into bed.
They cuddled up close
And Trix sleepily said:

"I love you, dear Midnight.
Please don't ever change.
You're truly a wonder,
A cat **sweet** and **strange**."

With that Midnight knew
What her friend said was true.
She thought, *I am special!*
And Trixie is too.

On pillows so soft,
Scented faintly with rose,
They drifted to sleep
Hand to paw, nose to nose.

A Note from Midnight:

Did you know that black cats like me are often the last to be picked from animal shelters? Sadly, it's true! People tend to choose cats with more unusual colours or markings. Sometimes black cats wait months — or even years — before finding a home.

So if you're thinking of getting a cat, keep in mind that black ones have just as much love to give. Some people even think we are lucky!

Remember to check out your local animal rescue centres, and give older cats a chance too. They can be just as playful as kittens!